In memory of Samuel J. Margolin, M.D.
—H.M.E.

For my favorite doctor, Bruce, and his
beautiful wife, Barbara. With love.
—L.R.

DR. DUCK

by **H. M. EHRLICH**
pictures by **LAURA RADER**

ORCHARD BOOKS • NEW YORK

Dr. Duck started early—
He's a very busy man.
He went to see patients
In a big, red van.

GOOD MORNING,
DR. DUCK!

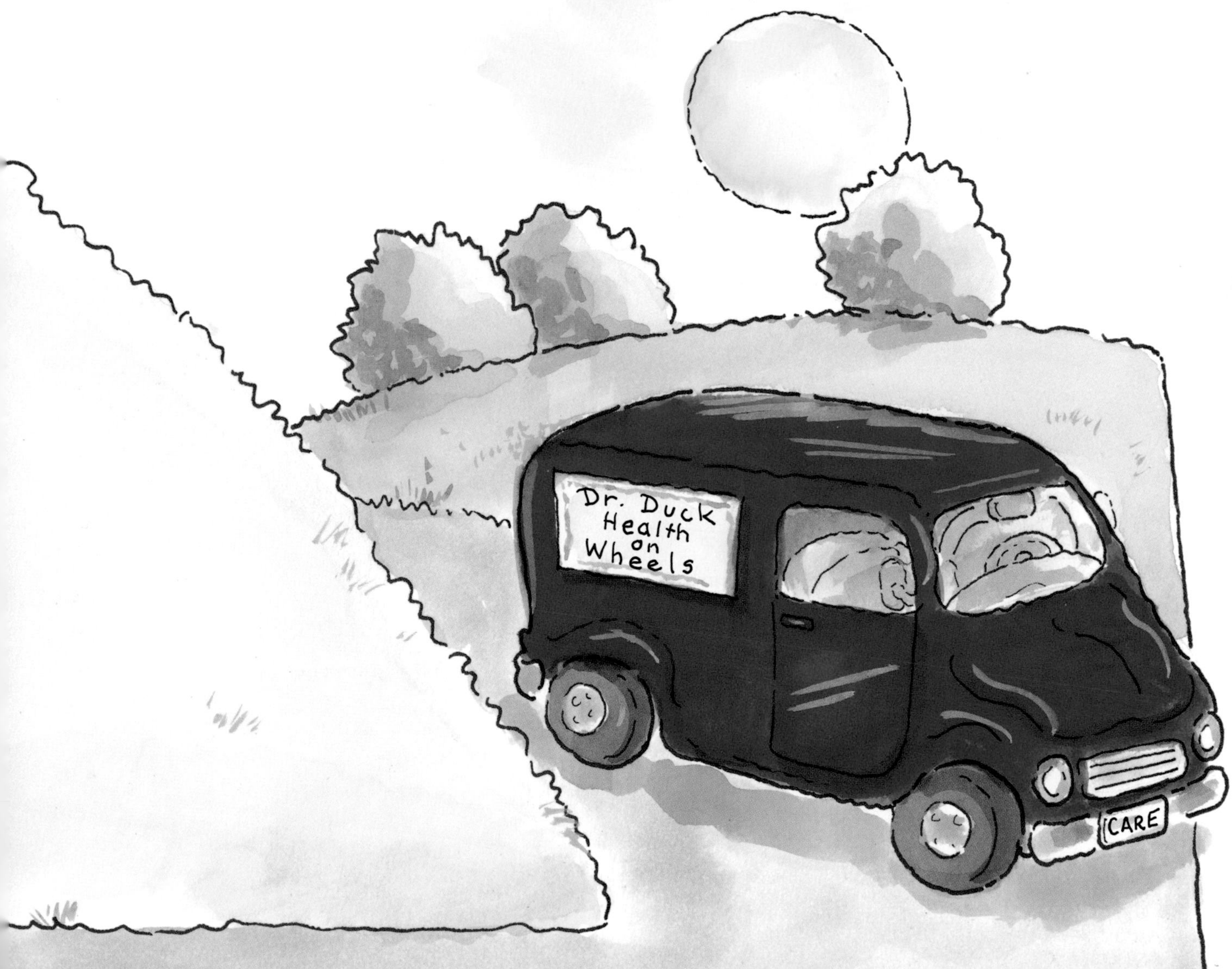

He ordered nose drops
For weasels with sneezles.

And looked down the throat
Of a rabbit with measles.

THANK YOU,
DR. DUCK!

He calmed Mother Mouse
Whose baby had fever.

And listened to the cough
Of a two-year-old beaver.

Cough syrup for a sheep
Who had a bad flu.

Pink pills for a cow
Too hoarse to moo.

A splint for a crow
With a broken toe.

An ice pack for a mule
Bumped by a hoe.

He checked a puppy
Who had the croup.

The doctor is IN

Please Watch Your Step

He examined a chicken
Who couldn't drink soup.

Three stitches for a moose
Whose antlers were loose.

He checked his throat
And felt his head.
"I think I'm ill,"
Dr. Duck said.

In came the rabbit,
In came the beaver,
They said Dr. Duck
Had a terrible fever.

The chicken clucked,
And Mrs. Mouse said,
"Get a soft pillow
To put under his head."

The puppy brought juice.
The moose brought tea.

The weasels tucked him in
As snug as he could be.

The skunks rushed in
And they began to cry,
"Oh, no, Dr. Duck,
Please don't die!"

Dr. Duck fell asleep,
Then woke up in a while.

He put on his vest
And gave them all a smile.

"It's the sickest I've been
In a long, long time.
But with friends like you,
Now I'm feeling fine."

HOORAY FOR DR. DUCK!